The Pickwick Club

Little Women

Louisa May Alcott

Retold by **Maggie Blossom**
Illustrated by **Katarzyna Bukiert**

Designed by Flowerpot Press
in Franklin, TN.
www.FlowerpotPress.com
Designer: Stephanie Meyers
Editor: Katrine Crow
ROR-0811-0114
ISBN: 978-1-4867-1268-7
Made in China/Fabriqué en Chine

10 Minute Classics

Good books are some of the greatest treasures in the world. They can take you to incredible places and on fantastic adventures. So sit back with a 10 MINUTE CLASSIC and indulge a lifelong love for reading.

We cannot, however, guarantee your 10 minute break won't turn into 15, 20, or 30 minutes, as these FUN stories and engaging pictures will have you turning the pages AGAIN and AGAIN!

Hello, dear reader, and welcome
to the tale of the four March sisters:
Meg, Jo, Beth, and Amy. I only get to share
a few of their adventures with you today, but I encourage you
to learn all about them when you find the time...

Meg was the oldest March sister. She was kind and responsible and a great
help to her mother. It sometimes seemed like she herself was a mom to the
other three.

Jo was second oldest.
Some may have said
Jo was a tomboy, but
Jo just felt she was an
independent-minded woman.

Beth was second youngest. She was quiet,
caring, and enjoyed making her sisters happy. Beth
was a talented musician and loved to play piano for her family.

Amy was the baby of the family. She loved beautiful things and she
was a wonderful artist, but sometimes she worried about appearances
too much!

The girls lived on the East Coast of America a long time ago, during the American Civil War. Their mother, Marmee, had a lot to do, as their father was away serving as a chaplain in the war. There was little he could give to help his Little Women, beyond his words of encouragement...

With Christmas just days away, the girls were excited to receive a letter from their father. They all gathered around the fire to hear Marmee read it aloud. At the end of the letter, their father wished his girls his love and reminded his Little Women to work hard and to do their best in all they do.

The letter inspired each girl in her own way.
Amy said she would try not to be selfish.
Meg vowed to work harder.
Jo promised to pay more attention to her duties at home and spend less time daydreaming of great adventures.
Beth just cried, wishing her father could be with them.

The girls woke Christmas morning to discover their mother was not home. The housekeeper, Hannah, explained that their mother had gone to see a woman who needed her. "You know your mother," Hannah reminded them, "She cannot refuse to help people in need."

When Marmee returned home, she told the girls she had been with the Hummels, a very poor family that lived nearby. Marmee asked the girls if they wanted to give the Hummels their Christmas breakfast.

The four Little Women's father would have been proud to see them packing up their food for the neighbors.

When they arrived at the Hummel house, they helped feed the children and light a fire to keep them warm. Mrs. Hummel beamed and said angels had come to save them.

That evening, the March sisters'
kindness was returned many times
over as their wealthy neighbor,
Mr. Laurence, had heard of their kind
act and sent them a Christmas feast,
complete with cake, fruit, bonbons,
fancy flowers, and even ice cream!

Wealthy Mr. Laurence had a grandson named Laurie. Laurie was an only child and had been raised by his grandfather ever since his parents died. Often, Laurie would watch the March family through his window, wishing he could have some company. Jo was the first of the Little Women to become friends with Laurie...

Jo had noticed Laurie looking out his window. One day, she decided to invite him to come out to play. She threw a snowball at him as he leaned out his window, and she yelled for him to join in the fun. Laurie could not come out in the cold, as he was recovering from being ill, but he invited Jo in for a visit. Jo was very happy to visit and offered to read to him while he regained his strength.

Jo discovered that Laurie's grandfather had a huge library, which Jo loved, and a beautiful piano, which Beth would play.

Soon, all the March girls were spending time with Laurie and grew to love their times at the Laurence home.

The Laurence home was a fun addition to their lives, but some of the girls' favorite times were when they held meetings of The Pickwick Club in their very own attic. The Pickwick Club was a rainy day society the sisters created so they could publish their own newspaper and share it aloud with one another. Often, they pretended to be different characters in the society.

In The Pickwick Club newspaper, the sisters would write stories, poems, jokes, and news. They shared much laughter while reading it aloud. Jo loved writing stories so much that she knew she wanted to make it her life's work.

One day, Jo invited Laurie to join them in their favorite game. While the other sisters feared Laurie would laugh at them, he instead added to the fun, leading to a deep friendship among the young neighbors.

The Pickwick Club

Life moved along as it does—and it should—and as the sisters grew older, they were pulled in different directions...

Meg got married.

Amy traveled overseas to pursue her art.

Beth was poor in health, and so she stayed home with Marmee.

While Jo was worrying about what to do with her life,
Marmee wisely said: "Jo, you have so many extraordinary
gifts; how can you expect to lead an ordinary life?
You're ready to go out and find a good use for your talent."

And that is just what she did.

Jo was brave and moved to New York on her own to pursue her writing. In New York, Jo's writing was a success. She made enough money from her writing to support herself and send money back to her family as well.

While in New York, Jo met a man named Professor Bhaer. Professor Bhaer challenged Jo not to just worry about making money, but to try and become the great writer he knew her to be. This was hard for Jo to listen to, but great for her to hear. They became close friends, and Jo was taken with the Professor's intelligence, kindness, and generosity.

When Jo eventually returned home, she knew it was Professor Bhaer's friendship she would miss more than anything else.

The story of our Little Women is a much longer tale, and there are many more adventures and stories for you to discover, but there are a few more things I can share with you now...

Meg learned to be giving and follow her heart.

Jo learned to work hard to attain her dream.
(And she married Professor Bhaer!)

Beth spread much love and kindness.

Amy learned there were more important things to life than worrying about herself. (And she married Laurie!)

And so you see, dear reader, as they grew older, many things changed for the March sisters, but one thing that never changed was the friendship and togetherness they shared as sisters, and as Little Women.